Forget-Me-Not

Maxine Trottier

illustrated by
Nancy Keating

Tuckamore Books
a Creative Publishers imprint

St. John's, Newfoundland and Labrador
2008

We gratefully acknowledge the financial support of the Canada Council for the Arts,
the Government of Canada through the Book Publishing Industry Development Program (BPIDP),
and the Government of Newfoundland and Labrador through the Department of Tourism, Culture
and Recreation for our publishing program.

Illustrations and book design © 2008, Nancy Keating
Layout by Todd Manning

Published by
TUCKAMORE BOOKS
an imprint of CREATIVE BOOK PUBLISHING
a Transcontinental Inc. associated company
P.O. Box 8660, St. John's,
Newfoundland and Labrador
A1B 3T7

Printed in Canada by:
Transcontinental Inc.

Printed on acid-free paper

Library and Archives Canada Cataloguing in Publication

Trottier, Maxine
    Forget-me-not / Maxine Trottier ; illustrated by Nancy Keating.

Target audience: For ages 6-12.
ISBN 978-1-897174-24-1

    1. World War, 1914-1918–Juvenile fiction. I. Keating, Nancy II. Title.

PS8589.R685F67 2008   jC813'.54   C2008-901891-5

For Brad, Braden,
Brady and Brittany
M.T.

For Rebecca,
Zachary and Malcolm
N.K.

The author would like to thank Nora Flynn of Granny Bates for her editorial expertise, Bert Riggs for historical details, Gene Flynn for boat wisdom, Chris Mills for lighthouse reference images, and Don Johnson of the Cape Bonavista Lighthouse Provincial Historic Site for his advice.

*B*ridget Keats had a spyglass and so she was a watcher of boats. She watched the men head out to sea each morning no matter the weather, their skiffs laden with line and nets and jiggers. She peered at schooners going by, as they leaned over in the wind, heavy with fish and salt and who could imagine what.

On very fine days, her mother sometimes sailed across the bay with her own cargo. Up to the post office she would walk, a canvas bag over her shoulder. In it were wool stockings for their soldiers fighting in the war.

"Your father would have gone, had the sea not taken him," Mother explained. "It's the least we can do for our boys."

Bridget would watch for her while she worked in the garden and while she hung out the wash. When she saw their punt, when it was just a little small white dot on the horizon, she would hoe the last weed or hang the last sheet. The glass in her apron pocket, she would run down to the wharf and meet her mother.

On certain days Bridget's mother brought back letters from away. Some people read them right there on the wharf, just like that. Not her mother. She and Bridget would take the letters home and Mother would read them aloud that night.

If the news were hard, and during the war it was sometimes very hard, they would wrap it up inside themselves. That's what you did with hard news, Bridget understood, especially news about the war. But if it were good news, news about their soldiers, that was different.

"'Dear Mrs. Keats,'" Mother would read. "'Thank you for the stockings you and Bridget sent us. We do love grey,'" and they'd both laugh. The next morning the good news would spread from kitchen to kitchen like the smell of fresh warm bread.

On windless days Bridget rowed her rodney over to a small, nearby island. An old lighthouse stood there, wildflowers growing where they could, sheltered by the rocks. No one had kept the light for a long while, her mother had said. The new light was a grand thing, but this one had guided her father and grandfather home. Its glass panes were crusted with salt; inside were old spider webs and the dry bodies of dead moths. Bridget would think about the sea and all it had taken, and how the war was doing the same. Her eyes closed, she would try to imagine the way it must sound when shells exploded and the men were wounded. How could anyone be that brave?

Then one day Bridget spied the merchant's boat at the island. When it sailed away it had left a chest on the stones. It had also left a man.

"His name is Jake Wiseman," Mother told her that night as she knitted. "Was an officer. Brought books and such in that chest."

"The boys say that only a coward would have come back. They say his face is a cruel sight." And Bridget shivered.

"He was sent back because he was wounded, poor man," Mother explained. She sighed. "You'll bring over food, Bridget, my love, but other than that you will leave him in peace."

Then came the day Bridget had to row to the island with her mother's bread and a basket of eggs. She tried to think of a reason she should not, and even thought to say she was ill, but in the end she went. And she nearly was ill, her stomach all in knots and her hands sweating on the oars. When Bridget got there, when she climbed the path and stood at the door of the keeper's house, her fear rose up like something terrible and she dropped everything.

That night Bridget dreamed of a full yellow moon rising over a far-away country. She stood alone on a sea of mud in a deep, deep ditch with soldiers sleeping all around her. The moon looked down and, in her father's voice, whispered to her.

Bridget thought of the dream the next time she rowed over to the island. She thought of it when she stopped to pick flowers for her mother, and when she climbed the path.

"Coward," her moon father had whispered.

A note was tacked to the door of the house. "I prefer my eggs unscrambled. J.W.," it said.

Bridget set down the basket very carefully. She thought a moment and then laid the bunch of flowers on it.

The next time she came, a new note had been left. So had a pencil that hung from a string.

"Sea lungwort," Bridget slowly read aloud. "What can that be?" she wondered. "If it is something you want," she wrote back, "we have none at home. Mother will have to row across the bay for it. Yours, Bridget Keats."

It was, she learned a few days later, a flower, the very flower she had picked.
"Sea lungwort," said his note. "Also known as ice plant. Not for sale, but
still beautiful. J.W." And there was the flower sketched beneath his words.

"We call it blue bonnet," she wrote back." There were yellow flowers growing in a sheltered bit of sunshine against the house. Bridget picked some of them and tucked them under the edge of the paper. "What do you call these?"

"Toadflax," he wrote. She'd always called them butter and eggs.

Each time she came, Bridget brought something different, certain he could not possibly know all the flowers, but he did.

"Bird vetch," he wrote. "Cinquefoil, lupine, bottle brush, alexanders." He began to give her the Latin names for the flowers, and what had been as ordinary as milk suddenly sounded magical.

"Roseroot," Bridget would whisper to herself at night in bed. "Sedum rosea."

When the wind was too strong for her to row across, Bridget watched the lighthouse through her spyglass. She saw nothing strange or terrible, only Jake Wiseman's shadowy form moving beyond the cloudy glass of the lighthouse. To her surprise, the windows began to sparkle and the old brass lamp gleamed. One night, for just a little while, light spilled from the lighthouse. Then it was gone.

A few days later, Bridget rowed across to the island. There on the shore she looked across the slick still water of the bay where the town shimmered as though it were a mirage. Her mother had delivered stockings that morning. Through the spyglass Bridget could see her starting for home, the punt's wake spreading out smoothly behind her. It was quiet, very quiet when she set down the basket and placed a bunch of flowers on it, flowers she had picked from their garden. There was only the chirping of an early cricket calling for autumn, and a soft wash of wavelets.

And then, a terrible roar.

Bridget turned as the town disappeared in the low clouds of the squall
that raced over the bay and swallowed her mother. Wind and slashing rain
hit the island.

"Help!" she screamed, pounding on the door. Her mother would never find her way in. She would be swept out to sea and lost. "Do something!"

There was no answer.

Bridget ran to the lighthouse, the wind screaming as she flung open the door and hurried up the steps. If she lit the lantern, if Mother saw it, but match after match sputtered out in her wet fingers. She dropped sobbing to the cold stones.

The wind shrieked in triumph and so she did not hear the footsteps, the striking of a match. Light poured across the room and out into the storm.

"She'll see it," he said quietly. "She'll find her way home."

Bridget raised her eyes and there was Jake Wiseman.

She was too young to think of what it must have cost him to show his face.
She could only think of her mother. "Thank you," Bridget whispered.

When the squall passed Jake Wiseman watched her run from the lighthouse. He saw her row across to the shore where her mother waited. He tended the light until dawn, thinking about those who watched for the sake of others, about what you kept and what you gave away. He thought about his comrades. He watched a perfect sunrise over the quiet ocean, and then Jake Wiseman put out the lamp.

The next morning someone told them there'd be no need for Bridget to go to the lighthouse again. The man was gone back to town, or to the mainland. Maybe even over to France again. Imagine.

Bridget rowed across anyway. The lighthouse was dark and so was the keeper's house, although the door was open a crack. She walked in. It was filled with the emptiness that is left behind when someone goes away. Nothing remained to show that the man had ever been there, except a sheet of paper on the house's rough table. Next to it was the bunch of flowers, the last she'd picked to test him.

"Forget me not, Bridget Keats," she read aloud. "Yours, Jake Wiseman."

*B*ridget would think of those flowers in later years, when she watched soldiers march by, when she heard the pipes and listened to the speeches. What ever happened to the man who had come here to find peace, she sometimes wondered. She hoped he had found it at last.

Newfoundlanders and Labradorians have always been strong folk. It takes strength, after all, to bring in the cod and to make the fish day after day. And it takes bravery. You have to be brave to hold together a life in a place where the sea can wash it all away and change everything, just like that.

It wasn't the sea that changed things one particular summer, though. On August 4, 1914, the United Kingdom declared war on Germany in the name of the British Empire. The Great War, they said it was in time, and it did seem great at first. Men willingly answered the call of the Newfoundland Patriotic Association to raise an army of five hundred soldiers. There would be reserve troops, as well, waiting to take their turn.

By September, thousands had volunteered and from them were chosen the first five hundred. This was the Newfoundland Regiment. Because of the blue strips of cloth they wore between knee and boot top as leggings, these soldiers were nicknamed the Blue Puttees.

They trained hard and while they trained, another sort of army rose up to support them. The Women's Patriotic Association knit socks and cuffs, and helped the Red Cross pack supplies. Funds were raised by the Society of United Fishermen and other groups. Everyone pitched in.

On the morning of July 1, 1916, the Newfoundland Regiment waited in trenches at a point called Beaumont-Hamel on the Somme River in France. They had trained at home and in England and Scotland, fought at Gallipoli in Turkey, and they were ready. The soldiers began their advance at 9:15 am. Within a half hour, it was over for them. When the roll was called the next day, only 68 of the 801 men were able to answer. When the terrible news reached home, the country mourned deeply. One year later, a commemoration service was held at St. John's to honour those who had fought. People wore forget-me-nots in remembrance.

Today Canada honours its veterans in many ways. Cenotaphs stand in cities and small towns; they guard the battlefields where soldiers once fought. But on each July 1, Newfoundland and Labrador pauses, for that day is Memorial Day. The flags are lowered to half-staff, solemn ceremonies are held, and for a moment, the province is silent. People wear forget-me-nots. They remember, and they say thank you.